USBORNE HOTSHOTS

VAMPIRES

USBORNE HOTSHOTS

VAMPIRES

Written by Caroline Young
Designed by Nigel Reece

Illustrated by Graham Humphreys, Barry Jones
and Rob Mc Caig

Series editor: Judy Tatchell
Series designer: Ruth Russell

Additional illustrations by Victor Ambrus,
Derick Bown, Chris Chaisty, Oliver Frey,
Terry Gabbey, Elaine Lee, Seonaid Mackenzie,
Harvey Parker, Ken Stott, Jenny Thorne
and Pat Thornton

CONTENTS

Vampire facts

Many kinds of vampires are described in this book; all of them drink blood. Whether or not you believe they really exist is up to you. You need to know some basic information about them before making up your mind, though.

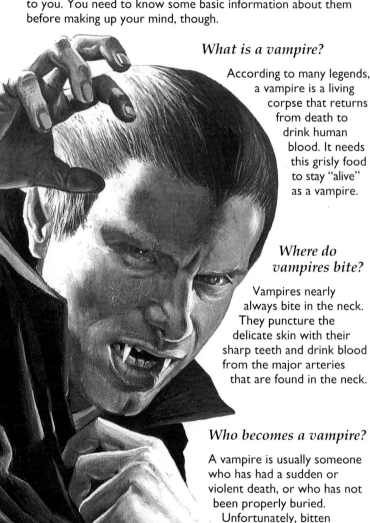

What is a vampire?

According to many legends, a vampire is a living corpse that returns from death to drink human blood. It needs this grisly food to stay "alive" as a vampire.

Where do vampires bite?

Vampires nearly always bite in the neck. They puncture the delicate skin with their sharp teeth and drink blood from the major arteries that are found in the neck.

Who becomes a vampire?

A vampire is usually someone who has had a sudden or violent death, or who has not been properly buried. Unfortunately, bitten victims become vampires once they die, too.

Can a vampire be killed?

Yes, but killing a vampire is a tricky job. Vampires can only be released from their quest for blood by following certain steps. You can find out what they are on page 7.

Are vampires dead?

Yes and no. Vampires are sometimes called "the undead", because their spirits are active inside a dead body. The fresh blood they drink keeps them looking alive.

Where are vampires usually found?

By day, a vampire stays in its grave, as a body that shows no signs of decay at all. By night, a vampire is likely to be prowling in search of a meal of blood. Then, they could be anywhere.

What does a vampire look like?

This varies a great deal, as the pages ahead will show. Some vampires were even said to be completely invisible, a bodiless "ghost". Most have sharp front side teeth for biting victims.

When are vampires most dangerous?

Vampires are at their most fearsome during the night. Most rise from their graves at sunset. They have until dawn, when the sun rises, to drink their fill and return to the grave.

How do vampires get out of their graves?

Some vampires are said to seep out of their graves like a mist and then re-form into a body above ground. Others have to dig their way out each night. Many just lift the coffin lid.

Do vampires only drink blood?

Some legends tell of vampires also eating the flesh of a dead person, or drinking the blood of animals. Human blood is the food they like best, though, according to most stories.

How can you keep vampires away?

There are several traditional "vampire deterrents". Whether they work is uncertain, but they are centuries old. You can find out what they are just by turning the page...

Bloodsucking beliefs

The ways people used to protect themselves from vampires seem a little strange to us now. In our technological age, we are less likely to fear becoming a vampire after we die. But hundreds of years ago, things were very different...

The plague carriers

A disease called the plague killed millions in medieval Europe. Nobody could find a cause for it, or a cure. Many people believed that vampires spread the disease and they lived in terror of attack. So  many died from the plague that wild animals often reached the bodies of the dead before there was time to bury them.

The gory remains of these attacks were often blamed on bloodthirsty vampires.

Mutilated bodies

People lit bonfires and rang church bells to fend off vampire  attack. They dug up suspected vampires and mutilated their bodies to make sure they did not rise again from the grave.

Vampires, keep off!

The best way to fend off a vampire was to show it a crucifix, the sign of the Christian religion. People believed that an evil vampire would fear the sign of God.

Garlic was hung over doors and windows to keep vampires away. As recently as 1973, a man choked to death on a clove of garlic he had put in his mouth to deter vampire attack.

Traditionally, vampires were not fond of wild roses. Draping the flowers around windows and doors was a good way to keep vampires at bay.

How to kill a vampire

Ways of killing a vampire varied, but all were incredibly bloodthirsty. The main method was to drive a stake through its heart with a single blow.

Alternatively, red-hot nails could be hammered into the vampire's head or its heart ripped out and boiled in oil. Many believed that beheading the body with a gravedigger's spade was the surest method.

Vampires hated bright lights, preferring the dark night. People lit torches outside their houses and roaring fires inside them, to protect themselves.

If an animal jumped over a corpse, people believed the animal would become a vampire. Animals were often smeared with garlic, and kept away from unburied corpses.

Bright sunlight and strong moonlight had the power to bring the dead back to life, many people believed. They kept curtains drawn around dead bodies before burial.

Dead or alive?

For centuries, burying people correctly was very important in the battle to get rid of vampires. Some elaborate rituals developed surrounding death and burial. We still carry out some of them today although the original reasons for doing so might have been forgotten.

Resting in peace

1. Flowers were said to help a spirit accept that it was dead, so flowers were laid on graves.

2. Graves were dug deep, so that the heavy earth piled on top of the coffins would keep the corpses in.

3. Graves were clearly marked, as walking over a grave might make the body into a vampire.

4. Heavy gravestones helped stop corpses from climbing out again.

Safety measures

When people dug up suspected vampires, or buried people they thought might become one, more rituals were followed.

Crosses made of willow were put under the corpse's arms and holy water was sprinkled over the grave. The corpse's mouth was crammed with garlic, which vampires hated.

Lastly, seeds were scattered around the churchyard. People believed that vampires had to stop and count the seeds, and this would take them so long that they wouldn't have time to kill before dawn.

Graveyard puzzles

For many people, the existence of bloodsucking creatures that rose from the dead seemed the only possible explanation for the strange sights they sometimes saw in graveyards.

When graves were found open soon after burial and bodies missing, people assumed that a vampire was at work. In fact, body snatchers had probably taken the corpses and sold them to doctors for medical research.

Alive?

The main "proof" of a vampire was that its body looked as if it was still alive when it was dead. A corpse that had not rotted or, stranger still, had a blush on its cheeks or long nails, was almost certainly a vampire, people believed.

If a body like this was found in an opened grave, it had to be "killed" in the most thorough of ways (see page 7).

People sometimes even opened graves to check their loved ones had not become "undead" vampires.

Catalepsy

A more likely cause of such lifelike "corpses" is a disease called catalepsy, which can leave victims seeming to be dead when they are in fact still alive. Their nails continue to grow and blood pumps through their veins, though breathing is hard to detect.

If the "dead" person later woke from their cataleptic trance, their fate was sealed indeed. They slowly suffocated.

In days when nobody knew about such ailments, sufferers were believed to be dead and were quickly buried to stop their corpses from spreading further disease.

Doomed

Ghastly examples of bodies twisted in their coffins and bloody fingernails caused by people trying in vain to push or claw their way out of their own graves were seen as awful proof of vampirism. Being buried alive is still a popular theme for horror stories.

The thirst for blood

Some of the goriest vampire stories of all come from Central and Eastern Europe. Several famous vampire tales were based on the bloodthirsty habits of real people living there.

Cruel rule

During the 1400s, Transylvania, a part of what is now Romania, was ruled by Prince Vlad Dracula. His bloodthirsty deeds probably inspired Bram Stoker's famous novel, *Count Dracula* (see pages 16-17).

Vlad was nicknamed "Vlad the Impaler" as he enjoyed impaling his enemies on wooden stakes. He also skinned, chopped and roasted people before feeding them to their families. Showing lack of respect to Vlad could leave you with your hat firmly nailed to your head, too.

Vlad was deposed and beheaded at the age of 46. Amazingly, he was regarded as a "cruel but just ruler" by many of his subjects during his reign. Many people thought he was a hero for driving enemy armies out of his kingdom. He was even buried in a monastery.

The story of Arnold Paole

In this famous story, Arnold Paole, a young Serbian soldier, was bitten by a vampire while fighting in Greece in 1729. He ate soil from its grave and smeared himself with its blood, hoping to avoid becoming a vampire himself. Then he returned home to live quietly in the village where he was born.

When he died in a farming accident, the villagers buried him in the churchyard with great sadness. Their grief soon turned to horror, though, when they saw him haunting their village.

Within a month, Arnold's spirit was killing people. When his grave was opened by village officials, everyone could see that Arnold had become a bloodsucking vampire. He looked alive, with fresh blood around his mouth.

Free of evil

Over the next 17 days, the villagers had to kill over 20 vampires that Paole had bitten. They drove stakes through their hearts, chopped off their heads and burned their bodies. Only then was the village free of the vampire's evil.

Beauty treatment

Countess Elizabeth of Bathory was another Eastern European ruler with a taste for blood. When she hit a maid one day, the poor girl's blood splashed over the Countess. Convinced that the blood made her skin look young again, Elizabeth started bathing in the blood of young girls every morning. Over the next ten years, she ordered about 650 girls to be killed. Their blood was then drained and gently warmed for the Countess to soak in. In 1611, her sickened courtiers shut her into one room of her castle, where she starved to death.

Vampires around the world

Vampires vary in different parts of the world. All of them need to drink blood to remain their ghastly selves, but some have particular tastes and habits.

 A Portuguese vampire called Bruxas becomes a bird each night. She is said to drink the blood of her own children in this vampire form.

Bulgarian vampires take 40 days after burial before they are ready to drink blood. Then, they look human but have only one nostril and, often, a long pointed tongue.

 Vietnamese vampires look like flying heads. They have specially-shaped noses to help them drink blood, rather like a vampire bat has.

Russian vampires or *vieszcy*, chew their own hands and feet while in their coffins during the day. They come out at night to cause havoc.

Japanese vampires might be the hardest to recognize. They are able to change their shape and size and can even take on the appearance of their dead victim to avoid discovery.

The German *Neuntoter* vampire stinks and its body is covered in sores, so people used to blame it for spreading the plague (see page 6).

Some Malaysian vampires are called *langsuirs*. They are women who return from death as owl-shaped vampires, and drink children's blood.

Another German vampire, the *Nachzehrer*, eats its burial shroud while in its coffin. It also keeps its left eye open at all times and makes grunting noises like a pig.

A Danish vampire, Mara, attacks sleeping young men. She is a beautiful woman by day but any man who loves her gets bitten.

Polongs are vampires which haunt Malaysian jungles. No bigger than a child's finger, they use an evil cricket to burrow a "drinking-hole" in the victim's skin.

A Brazilian vampire called a *jaracaca* is shaped like a snake. It drinks milk as well as blood, often from a mother's breast as she feeds her baby, unaware of the vampire's presence.

13

Vampires of the East

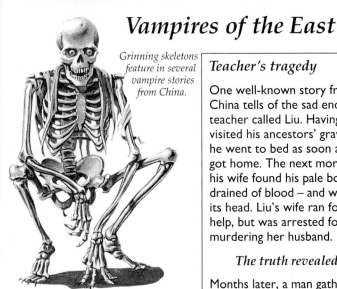

Grinning skeletons feature in several vampire stories from China.

Vampire stories from China seem to be particularly grisly. Some stories even tell of people's souls lingering on Earth after they have died so that they can turn their own bodies into vampires.

Threat after death

Many people used to believe that any corpse that did not begin to rot straight after death must be a vampire. Even part of a body, such as a skeleton or a skull, was at risk from being possessed by devils and becoming a vampire.

People believed that evil spirits were all around, waiting for a victim. Their fear of becoming a bloodsucker was very real.

Teacher's tragedy

One well-known story from China tells of the sad end of a teacher called Liu. Having visited his ancestors' graves, he went to bed as soon as he got home. The next morning, his wife found his pale body drained of blood – and without its head. Liu's wife ran for help, but was arrested for murdering her husband.

The truth revealed

Months later, a man gathering wood noticed an open grave with a coffin lying nearby. He fetched friends and they peered inside. A hideous vampire lay with Liu's head in his hands.

The man reported his discovery to the authorities. The vampire looked alive, but it had fangs instead of teeth and its body was covered in hair. It was burned, Liu's head was buried with his body, and his innocent wife was released.

Ch'iang Schich

Some of the most spine-tingling tales from China concern murderous walking corpses called Ch'iang Schichs. In one story about such a creature, four men arrived at an inn for the night. Their room had five beds, but one was hidden behind curtains.

One of the men could not sleep, and saw the curtains part and the pale corpse of a young woman stagger toward his sleeping friends. As she breathed over each man, he died at once. The fourth man held his breath in terror, which saved his life.

Narrow escape

The man ran out into the night. The Ch'iang Schich pursued him, its sharp claws outstretched. As the exhausted man fell back against a tree, the creature's claws struck at him. The man fainted and slid down the trunk, out of its grasp.

When he came to, it was dawn. The lifeless monster was hanging above him, its claws still embedded in the tree...

Count Dracula

The best-known vampire tale is *Count Dracula*, written in 1897 by Bram Stoker. It is as famous today as it was when it was first published.

Bram Stoker was inspired to write his dark tale of the vampire Count by a horrific nightmare. This led him to research vampire legends from the Middle Ages and read about Vlad the Impaler's bloodthirsty habits (see page 10).

Stoker found out that Vlad's father's name was Dracul, which means "devil" or "dragon" in Romanian. Vlad was called Dracula, which means "son of Dracul". The writer had found a name to suit his vampire Count...

The Dracula story

In Stoker's novel, Count Dracula lives in a rambling castle in Transylvania, in Eastern Europe. His ambition is to move to England and spread vampirism. He employs a young lawyer called Jonathan Harker to arrange his move to England.

Harker arrives at Dracula's castle in Transylvania and soon realizes that the Count is a vampire and up to no good. But Harker's cleverness proves his undoing; Dracula imprisons Harker in the castle before the lawyer can alert anyone, and sets sail for England.

On the ship Dracula kills the crew and drinks their blood. Once in England he bites a girl called Lucy Westenra, making her a vampire. She roams London attacking people until a vampire expert, Dr. van Helsing, drives a stake through her heart.

Harker eventually escapes from Transylvania and follows Dracula to England. There he helps van Helsing search for the Count, who now includes Harker's wife among his victims. They track him back to Transylvania, and plunge a stake into his heart.

Dracula on film

Count Dracula is a rich source of material for film directors. Many variations on the story have been filmed, as well as numerous comedies about vampires and crazy counts.

Nosferatu

Stoker's novel was first filmed in 1922. The film was called *Nosferatu*, which means "the undead" in Romanian. Some of its spooky photographic effects (see left) made cinema history.

Classic Dracula

In 1927, a Romanian actor named Bela Lugosi began playing the Count on stage. He made a classic film in the role in 1931, and was buried in his black satin "Dracula" cloak when he died in 1956.

Hammer horror

In the late 50s, 60s and early 70s, the British actor Christopher Lee made films in the role of the evil Count, emphasizing his wily intelligence. Many people have associated Lee with Dracula ever since.

Christopher Lee as Dracula in a 1972 film.

Vampire appeal

The story seems to keep its appeal for film fans, as another film version appeared in 1979.

Then, in 1992, the director Francis Ford Coppola filmed the story with Winona Ryder, Anthony Hopkins and Keanu Reeves among the cast. This version began with Vlad the Impaler vowing to live a life of evil (see page 10 for more about him).

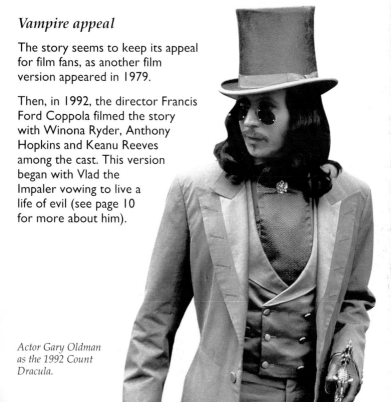

Actor Gary Oldman as the 1992 Count Dracula.

Vampire tales

There are countless vampire tales from around the world. Many, like these three, have been passed down through the generations.

Vengeful vampire

In a Russian tale set around 1800, an elderly politician forces a beautiful young woman to marry him. Worried about other men spending time with his wife, he keeps her locked in her chamber, miserable and alone. When the politician falls ill and realizes that he is going to die, he makes his wife swear never to marry again. If she does, he tells her he will return as a vampire to drink her blood.

Visitor

The old man dies, and his wife agrees to marry a young admirer. But on the night her marriage is announced, terrible screams tear the night air.

Servants find the young woman unconscious in her room. She is covered in bruises and blood is oozing from two tiny holes in her neck. Out of the castle windows, the servants glimpse a ghostly carriage rumbling over the drawbridge...

Repeat performance

Night after night, the woman is attacked by an unseen intruder who drinks her blood. Servants and guards find they feel strangely drowsy at the time of each attack, and fail to protect her. One night, guards stop the spectral coach as it leaves the castle and recognize the dead politician sitting within.

The curse is broken

The man's corpse is dug up and a wooden stake driven through its heart. The curse is broken, and the young woman is free to marry the man of her choice.

The vampire of Croglin Grange

This English tale is set in a house called Croglin Grange, in Cumberland. Two brothers and a sister are renting the house. One hot summer night, as the sister goes to bed, she is horrified to see a ghastly shape shuffling across the lawn. Its eyes blaze and its skin is brown and wrinkled. When it reaches her window, it begins scratching at the glass, then picks away at the lead that holds the glass in place.

Bitten

Terrified, the girl watches the creature push the glass out of the window and climb through. It flings her onto the bed.

As its teeth sink into her throat, she shrieks and her brothers rush to her room. One chases the creature over the lawn toward the family vault, shooting it in the leg before it disappears.

Vampire in the vault

All the tenants of the estate gather as the vault is opened the next day. Inside, a ghastly sight meets their eyes. Open coffins and mangled corpses litter the

floor. Only one coffin remains unopened. When the brothers lift the lid, they see the wizened creature within, a pistol-shot wound in its leg. According to tradition, they burn the vampire's corpse immediately.

The tale of Mr Ch'ien

In one Chinese story, a man called Mr. Ch'ien is riding home one night after a party in the town of T'ung Ch'eng. His route takes him across a graveyard, but the wine he has drunk dulls his fear. Suddenly, a ghastly figure rises up out of the earth in front of his horse. It leaps toward him, its long, matted locks flying and its face as white as chalk.

Ch'ien hits the figure hard and sees its head spin around on its neck. As it scurries away, its face looks back at Chi'en. The next morning, Ch'ien's hand is as black as ink. It stays that way for several years, a weird reminder of his encounter with a vampire that may have still been learning how to kill...

Animal vampires

In many legends, vampires appear as animals, with few obvious signs of their bloodthirsty nature.

Vampire bats

No spooky scene seems complete without bats. Vampire bats live hidden away in caves in Central and South America and, like most bats, only come out at night.

Vampire bats do drink blood, but they only attack humans if they are very hungry. They prefer animal blood and never take enough to kill their victim. The bats pierce the skin of their victim with sharp fangs, then lap up blood with their tongues. These drinking habits sound grisly, but in fact their bite is so painless that the animal often stays asleep while the bat takes its meal of blood. However, a bat's bite can pass on rabies and other diseases.

Terrible tales

Sometimes, people believed that the spirits of dead relatives expected some blood from the living as an offering. For instance, the Fan tribe of central Africa believed that a ghastly spirit with the head of an elephant haunted them. Unless it was satisfied by a blood offering, it would spread disease and death.

Beastly bajang

Malaysian vampire legends are plentiful. Some of the most vivid ones tell of a creature called a *bajang*, which usually takes the form of a polecat or a lizard. Anyone who had fits or fainted was thought likely to have been attacked by a *bajang*. The only way to free the victim from the vampire's grasp was to kill the magician or witch controlling it.

Animal disguises

In Transylvania, now Romania, people believed that a person's soul could very easily enter an animal, both before and after death. The most fearful form this could take would be the soul becoming an animal vampire called a *murony*.

A *murony* could disguise itself as a cat, dog, toad or any insect that drank blood, such as a mosquito. Transylvanians believed that they would only know a *murony* in its human form if they opened a grave and found a body with long, sharp nails and blood dripping from its eyes, ears, nose and mouth. In its animal form, its true vampire nature was better disguised.

Werewolves

A vampire was just one of the dangers people believed they faced during the Middle Ages. Closely related to them were werewolves, creatures addicted to eating both flesh and blood.

Some people said that even if you killed a werewolf, it would then live on as a vampire.

What were werewolves?

According to most legends, werewolves were people who turned into ravenous man-eating wolves at night.

Some hid their hairy wolf-skin beneath their human skin, and were said to "turn themselves inside out" to become a werewolf. Others turned into creatures that looked partly human and partly wolf.

Superstitions

As horrific reports of werewolves spread across Europe, many innocent people were accused of being one. Anyone who had one or several of these features was a suspect:

Bushy eyebrows that joined.

Small, pointed ears.

Third finger as long as the middle one.

Hairy palms of the hands.

Sometimes, unfortunate suspects were whipped to death, as their accusers tried to expose the wolf hair beneath their skin. Even if no evidence of them being a werewolf was found, they usually died.

Becoming a werewolf

Stories say that although many people became werewolves as a result of a curse, or extreme bad luck, some actually wanted to become one. To do this they had to follow certain steps. There are many versions of this strange process; here's just one of them.

A budding werewolf waited until a night when there was a full moon to begin the ceremony. Then he put bat's blood, wolfsbane, foxgloves, opium and blood into a cauldron.

When the mixture had boiled, the would-be werewolf smeared it into his skin. He then draped a wolf-skin around himself and asked evil spirits to make him a werewolf.

If the spells and the ritual worked, the man would become a werewolf by night. He would have to kill people and eat their flesh. Each morning he would return to his human form.

Wolf attack!

Many of the best-known werewolf tales come from France. Here are just three of them.

The King acts

During the 1760s, the village of Le Gévaudan in southern France was plagued by attacks from a wolf-like creature. Louis XV, the king of France at the time, sent three separate military forces to Le Gévaudan between 1765 and 1767 with orders to find and kill the wolf-creature. In 1767, they succeeded, and the corpse was paraded around the area. However, some eyewitness reports from the time say that the corpse had hooves rather than wolf's paws...

Wolf-woman?

Another famous werewolf legend concerns a hunter who is attacked by a wolf in the forest. He slashes at it with his sword, and cuts off the creature's forepaw, putting it into his bag as the wounded wolf lopes off.

When he gets home, he pulls out the wolf's paw from his bag, only to discover that it was changing into a woman's hand. With growing horror, the hunter recognizes the ring on one of the fingers... it belongs to his wife.

Realization

He rushes up to his wife's room, to find her lying dead on the bed. Her body is covered with deep sword cuts, and her right arm is a handless, bleeding stump.

Wolf-boy

One of the most famous werewolf tales surrounds the ghastly eating habits of a boy called Jean Grenier, who was 13 years old in 1604 when he was put on trial for murder and cannibalism. Jean said that someone called "The Lord of the Forest" had turned him into a werewolf and given him his taste for human flesh. The boy said he had eaten more than 50 children in the last three years.

Jean said that he had even snatched small babies from their cradles and eaten them. He especially enjoyed little girls, he confided in the court.

Boy or beast?

For instance, one afternoon, three girls had come upon Jean at the edge of the forest. His hair was filthy, his skin burned dark by the sun. His teeth and nails looked more like fangs and claws. He said that at sunset, he would eat them. This made them run for home, terrified.

Jean then bragged to a girl called Marguerite Poirier about his achievements as a werewolf and she told her parents. When Marguerite was later attacked by a creature she described as looking like a wolf, her parents ordered Jean's arrest.

The trial

At his trial in Bordeaux, Jean confessed to killing and eating people. Doctors said that he was suffering from a disease called lycanthropy. This leads people to imagine that they are werewolves. The judge sent him to a monastery but Jean did not change his ways. He still craved raw meat and ran on all fours. He always maintained he was a werewolf.

More beastly legends

Vampires and werewolves are the best known bloodsuckers, but by no means the only ones. There are many stories of people turning into other ferocious beasts. Here are just a few.

Fierce warriors

The armies of the Norse peoples, such as the Vikings, plundered Europe without mercy over a thousand years ago. The fiercest of their warriors were known as *berserkers*, which meant "dressed in bearskins".

The *berserkers* put on skins of animals such as wolves and bears before battle. Some people said that they actually became these wild beasts.

Fighting frenzy

The *beserkers* whipped themselves up into a frenzy of aggression before they began fighting. This wildness combined with their long hair, rough beards and ear-splitting battle-cries must have made them absolutely terrifying to their foes.

We still refer to them when we use the phrase "going berserk", which means acting as if you are completely out of control.

Punishment

According to Norse legend, Odin, the god of war, gave the *berserkers* their wild courage. Odin would punish a cowardly *berserker* by turning him into a grunting wild boar.

Wily werefox

An unusual tale from China and Japan describes bloodthirsty "werefoxes". These wily creatures could turn themselves into humans to trick and then kill people. Only foxes that had reached the advanced age of 500 and lived in a graveyard had this ability, though.

Werefox

Werebeasts

Humans that become animals are called werebeasts. In many parts of the world, there are tales of people turning into the most feared animal in that area.

For instance, in India, there are stories of weretigers. In South America, cunning werejaguars wait to catch you off guard. Werecrocodiles are said to lurk in North African rivers.

Werejaguar

Weretiger

Werecrocodile

Justice?

In Germany, a cruel bishop named Hatto was said to have extracted taxes from poor peasants until they starved. One legend tells of some of the peasants he had murdered turning into ravenous wererats and gnawing him to death.

Welsh witchery

People in Wales used to believe that witches became werewolves when they died. Some stories said that witches could disguise themselves as hares and drink milk from cows before the farmer had a chance to milk them.

29

Dracula mask

Count Dracula has pale skin, jet black hair, sharp fangs and piercing, evil eyes. You can disguise yourself as a vampire like him with this menacing mask. It is shaped onto a clay base which you can use again and again for different masks.

You will need:
• Shallow bowl, about 15cm (6in) wide
• 1kg (2lb) self-hardening clay
• Kitchen foil • Tray • Clingfilm
• White tissue paper, cut into squares
• Black and red paints • Black yarn
• Small sponge • Thin elastic
• Household glue (PVA)

Red paint on the end of the fangs looks like blood.

Glitter paint makes Dracula's evil eyes sparkle.

Facial features

Make these for step 4 opposite.

Flatten two marble-sized clay balls into the eye sockets for eyes.

Smooth two arched, sausage-shaped eyebrows into place.

Shape two more sausage shapes into lips. Make the top lip slightly longer, and shape a curve in it. Add fangs.

Smooth a clay wedge into the middle of the face for a nose. Smooth a small ball onto each side, for two nostrils. Poke your finger in to shape them.

1. Put the bowl upside down on the back of the tray and cover with clingfilm. Roll three orange-sized balls of clay.

2. Flatten the balls to cover the bowl. Add a larger ball to make the mask's chin. Smooth the joins with your thumbs.

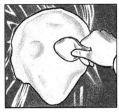

3. Halfway down the face, press in eye sockets with the back of a spoon. Rock the spoon from side to side as you press.

4. Shape Dracula's features (see box left) and press them on the face. Leave it in a warm place overnight to dry.

5. Lay foil over the face. Smooth it into the features with the sponge. If the foil rips, glue a patch over the tear.

6. Paint glue all over the mask, then stick on small squares of tissue paper. Cover the mask with four layers of tissue paper.

7. When dry, ease the mask off the clay base. Trim it, leaving a 1cm (½in) rim. Now turn the rim in and press it in firmly.

8. Poke eyeholes with a pencil. Poke a hole in each side of the mask and thread elastic through. Use black yarn for hair.

9. Use a nearly dry brush to shade the eye sockets red. Then paint the eyes as shown, the lips red and the brows black.

Index

Acknowledgements
Photographs on pages 18-19: the Kobal Collection.

This book is based on material previously published in the Usborne *Book of the Haunted
World*, Supernatural Guides: *Vampires, Werewolves and Demons*, Library of Fear, Fantasy and
Adventure: *Dracula*, *How to Draw Ghosts, Vampires and Haunted Houses*, *Book of Masks*.

First published in 1996 by Usborne Publishing Ltd, Usborne House, 83-85 Saffron Hill,
London EC1N 8RT, England.